My Journey to Becoming

THE MONKEY WHISPERER

My Life Inside the Exotic Animal Industry

By

Jim Hammonds

Foreword by Pam and Roger Rosairezoppe

LCCN:

2025914839

COPYRIGHT NUMBER:

1-14960978081

ISBN:

978-1-968973-03-2

Dedication

I would like to dedicate this book to my loyal customer base. Over the years, some of you have expressed curiosity about my background, so here it is, laid out for you. I can never thank you enough for your continued support and business.

With many of you, our relationship grew beyond transactions. I became friends with some of you, worked with your kids, and even your parents. Those connections have meant so much to me.

I'm sorry if I seemed distracted in recent years. I was dealing with an intense and draining battle with PETA. To protect myself and my family, I made the difficult decision to voluntarily rehome my animals. They were not seized, this was a decision I made in order to neutralize the threat.

I wish each of you the very best with your own animals. May they bring you as much happiness as mine brought to me.

I would also like to dedicate this book to my mother. Mom, you've stood by me through both my victories and my failures. Your unwavering loyalty, your compassion, and your willingness to simply listen have made my world a warmer and safer place. Your love has never gone unnoticed, and it has never been taken for granted.

I love you dearly.

Acknowledgment

I would like to acknowledge a few people who have supported me on the journey that led to this book.

First, my heartfelt thanks to the Rosairezoppe family, Roger, Pam, Dallas, and baby Rocco. They are dear friends who have witnessed my struggles, especially my battles with a certain political fringe group (PETA). Roger and Pam have shared their wisdom with me, and that has been truly invaluable.

I would also like to recognize Jamie and Nancy Banes. What began as a business relationship grew into a deep and lasting friendship. They are among the most compassionate animal keepers I've ever known, with a profound love for all animals. Their support over the past ten years means the world to me.

Kim also deserves special mention. Kim is incredibly knowledgeable and has endured scrutiny from regulatory agencies, just like I have, often over nothing. Despite it all, she has remained supportive and consistently offered sound advice. Thank you, Kim.

Last but certainly not least, I want to thank my mom. I wish everyone, especially my kids, could experience the love and support of a mom like mine. She has made my life immeasurably better through her caring heart, compassion, understanding, and loyal presence. She is always supportive, always listening, and always there. Thank you so much for being my mom. I love you!

About the Author

I was born in Portsmouth, Ohio, and was raised in a very rural community until I was 10 years old. At that time, my father was killed in Peebles, Ohio.

It was at this time that my mother took me and my two brothers to live in Columbus, Ohio, which was a drastic change, going from a very rural community to an urban environment. It took a lot of adjusting. All my life, I have been interested in animals. I was always a kid dragging home a puppy or a kitten. I was always out in the summertime, snake hunting, and looking for animals in the creeks and meadows around my home. I have two honorable discharges from the military, of which I am proud. I have four children: RACHEL, Jennifer, JUSTIN, and Dakoda. I also have seven grandchildren and one great-grandchild. I spent two decades in the exotic animal industry, dealing with people from coast to coast. I saw the good, the bad, and the ugly—mostly a very enjoyable experience. I got to interact with some amazing animals, and I met some really good and decent people. For the last five years of my career, I was pretty much harassed by the organization PETA. They tormented my family over minor paperwork infractions. We had never been accused, nor has it ever been alleged, that we mistreated an animal or kept it in any way other than in a clean and large enclosure. A lot of these animals were our personal pets.

I have voluntarily given up my animals now due to the unending harassment from PETA. I never got into this business to be in a legal quagmire all the time and endure its inevitable financial drain. This is a lunatic fringe political group that is seeking to impose its bizarre ideas on animal interaction on the general public! Their overriding goal is to make CRIMINALS OUT OF ANIMAL KEEPERS! I am now moving to the next chapter of my life. I am opening up a wedding venue and want to spend more time with my family and my grandkids. If you were one of my customers, thank you so much for your support. I really appreciate it.

Foreward

My name is Pam Rosairezoppe. My husband's name is Roger Zoppe. We are retired seventh-generation circus performers and animal keepers. I was born in England, where my grandfather and grandmother, known as "The Count" and "The Countess," founded Circus Rosaire in 1920. My father followed in their footsteps, as did my husband and I, continuing the legacy with our chimp act. Roger Zoppe was also a famous horse bareback rider.

Together, we've traveled the world with our circus and chimpanzee show. Over the years, we've had the honor of performing at the White House twice and have appeared on The Tonight Show with Johnny Carson, Captain Kangaroo, Bozo the Clown Show, and Amazing Animals. We've also performed for royalty around the world.

I met Jim Hammonds, also known as "The Monkey Whisperer," several years ago when he was looking for some ringtail lemurs. At the time, I had several. From the moment we met, my family and I sensed a kindred spirit in Jim. We quickly became good friends with him, his wife, and their boys, Dakoda and Justin.

My family and I have visited their home on several occasions. Jim's animals are always healthy and clearly well-cared for. The cleanliness of his facility is consistently impressive.

Jim has a special connection with animals—it's his passion. He has extensive experience, especially when it comes to nurturing baby animals. It's not uncommon to see him running errands or handling daily tasks with a baby monkey in tow, so he can keep a close eye on them.

We have watched as Jim has been unfairly targeted by PETA over minor paperwork issues. Not once has there ever been an allegation of abuse or mistreatment. Unfortunately, this kind of harassment has become common. Animal keepers everywhere are being aggressively pursued by PETA, which seems determined to force their misguided views on everyone. If you disagree with them, you're demonized through press releases and negative articles.

I am saddened by the state of our industry today. The overregulation and the way PETA has influenced young people into believing that human-animal interaction is harmful is disheartening. Their false narratives unfairly paint animal keepers in a negative light. In truth, people could learn far more about animals from those who dedicate their lives to caring for them than from fringe political groups that lack real experience.

I truly hope that in the future, the public will see animal keepers for who they really are—caring, knowledgeable individuals with a deep love for the creatures in their care.

Thank you,

Pam Rosairezoppe

The Monkey Whisperer
Jim Hammonds
727-743-7178

Table of Contents

Chapter 1
The Chaos of Appalachia

I remember the day I learned what death looked like. It was March of 1974, and everything changed. I was ten years old. My father, Jack, had been beaten so badly by his girlfriend's father that he was hospitalized. That's not what I remember most about that day, though. What I remember most is walking into that hospital parking lot and seeing my grandparents. They were wailing, looking up at the sky, unable to hold back the grief. I didn't need to ask what had happened. I knew at that moment that my dad was dead.

You see, I'd never seen death before. I had no idea what it meant to lose someone close. But in that moment, I felt it like a punch to the gut, a weight that fell on me and stayed there. That was the start of everything falling apart. After that, my life became a series of changes, each one more jarring than the last.

I was born in 1963 in Portsmouth, Ohio, a place that—at the time—was one of the poorest parts of the country. Even today, the area is a part of Appalachia, known for its tough, gritty, and impoverished roots. It's the same area Vice President JD Vance hails from, though I didn't know him then. I just knew that everything we had was hard-earned, and most of what we had was not enough.

I come from a family where survival was more of a daily question than a certainty. My father was a livestock breeder—a cattleman, they called him—and my mother,

Joanne, was a homemaker. I was the eldest of three boys, with a younger brother, David, John, and a sister who came later. My parents' marriage was a battleground, and I grew up surrounded by the sounds of arguing, the smell of whiskey, and the confusion of trying to understand why we couldn't ever seem to find peace. My dad was an alcoholic and a womanizer. The chaos he caused left deep scars on all of us.

We moved around a lot. I don't know if it was because it was easier for my dad to leave town when things got tough or if it was because we were so poor that it was cheaper to move than to stay. But we never stayed in one place long enough to build any roots. When my parents split, I was caught in the middle. My dad had more money than my mother, so he got custody of me and my brothers, and we moved to my grandfather's farm in Cherry Fork, Ohio.

That's when things got even worse. We weren't allowed to see our mother, and for almost a year, we lived without her. I was angry, confused, and resentful. My brothers and I spent those months trying to make sense of a world that kept shifting beneath our feet.

In March 1974, life dealt a blow I never saw coming. My dad had a girlfriend, Carol, and her father beat him so badly that he had to be hospitalized. That moment would forever change my life.

My dad spent a week in the hospital, and when the time came, my uncle drove us to see him. As we pulled into the parking lot, I saw my grandparents and my other uncle wailing, their cries echoing through the air as they looked up at the sky. I had never seen them like that before.

And in that instant, without anyone saying a word, I knew—my dad was gone. I had never faced death before, but from that moment on, nothing would ever be the same. When my father died, everything we had ever known fell apart. My mother, the woman who had fought so hard for us, showed up with the sheriff and took us away from our grandfather's farm. I still remember the look on his face when I left. He had a look of intense, unrestrained anger. We were taken from the countryside and thrown into the heart of Columbus, Ohio. The city was a whole new world, one I didn't know how to navigate.

We were immersed in poverty—the kind that made you feel invisible. I remember standing in line at school, waiting for lunch, and having to say the word "Free" when the cashier asked. It felt like a spotlight shining down on me, exposing everything I didn't want to admit. Some days, I couldn't bring myself to say it. I just skipped lunch altogether.

I grew my hair long in an attempt to adjust to the city, to try to fit in. But it was hard. The culture shock was immense, and the city felt like a jungle I didn't know how to survive in.

One day, my brother John and I found ourselves on the banks of the Ohio River. We spotted an old gas tank and thought it would be fun to float on it. The rusted metal didn't hold up, though, and we nearly drowned. A man in a small boat came by and rescued us, but it felt like a close brush with death. It made me realize how fragile life could be.

When I was 12, another big shift came. My mother met a man in Columbus, Ohio. This man would become my stepfather, but he was just another version of the same story. Another alcoholic, another womanizer, who abandoned us when my mother was pregnant with my sister. So, we were left to survive on the charity of his family. My mother worked at a truck stop, bartending for a few bucks just to make ends meet.

At 13, I got my first job as a dishwasher at the Country House Restaurant. It was a far cry from the farm life I had known, but it was something I could hold onto. It was the first time I felt like I was contributing, even if just a little.

Looking back on all of this, I realize I didn't have the luxury of innocence. My childhood was chaos, full of pain and loss, but it also shaped me into someone who knows how to survive. When you come from nothing, you learn to hold on to whatever scraps life gives you. And for me, those scraps became the foundation of everything that came after.

Chapter 2
Hello Virginia

In 1977, we arrived in Abingdon, Virginia. At first, it felt like a fresh start, but that didn't last long. After just six months, my mom's third husband abandoned us. She was pregnant with my sister at the time, and suddenly, we were left drifting, not knowing what to do or where to go next.

Determined to keep us afloat, my mom rented a house in Bristol, Virginia, and found a job at a truck stop. That was our new beginning. My siblings and I started attending John Battle High School, which was just up the road from where we lived. I knew our financial situation wasn't great, so I started doing odd jobs whenever I could. There was no illusion about it—I needed to work if I wanted to have any money.

That's when my stepdad's mother offered me a job at a country restaurant. It was my first real job and the first paycheck I ever received. But I was too young to work legally, so I had to step outside whenever inspectors came by until they were gone. Despite that minor inconvenience, I loved working there. The place was filled with young people, and after the restaurant closed for the night, we would sit by the fire during the winter, drink alcohol, and smoke weed. Everyone was older than me, but they treated me like one of their own.

One funny memory that sticks with me involved two step-sisters who worked there as waitresses. Both were named Kim—one was a blonde, and the other was a brunette.

They were gorgeous and, unfortunately, quite jealous of each other. One day, they started arguing about who was the better kisser. They turned to me and asked if I could settle the debate. That was the moment I felt like I had died and gone to heaven. They would take turns French kissing me in a private room at the restaurant, hoping I would choose one over the other. This went on for a week until they figured out I was dragging it out just to keep the fun going. Once they caught on, the game ended—to my disappointment. I ran into one of them years later, and we laughed about it.

It was around this time, when I was 16, that I met the girl who would become my wife. Melissa was completely different from me. She was a good girl from a working-class family—no drinking, no drugs. She was a cheerleader at a neighboring high school. I couldn't believe she liked me, but somehow, we clicked. For the next two years, we were a steady couple. We spent most of our time hanging out, partying, and going on double dates with our friends Rob and Nancy. Rob had a car, which made him the designated driver most of the time. Sometimes, Melissa could borrow her parents' car, but Rob was usually the one behind the wheel. For about a year and a half, we did nothing but cruise around, smoke weed, drink, and have fun. Those were good days.

But while the fun lasted, I knew I was coming of age and needed to think about my future. I didn't have much of a plan, so I decided to quit high school and enlist in the U.S. Navy. It felt like the right move, even though it meant I would leave everything behind. My drinking only got worse in the Navy because it was the perfect environment for it. I became what you'd call a "functional alcoholic."

Leaving for boot camp was a huge step. I had never been on an airplane before, but the military paid for my flight from Knoxville, Tennessee, to Chicago, Illinois. When I arrived, they put us up in a hotel for the night, and of course, I had been drinking heavily. The following day, before daylight, we were put on a bus and taken to the Great Lakes Naval Training Center. That was a rude awakening.

As soon as we arrived, the yelling began. The instructors spoke to us in ways I had never been spoken to before. They humiliated us, calling us names and breaking us down. It was a crash course in discipline, something I had never really experienced. I struggled to adjust, but in some strange way, it was helping me. Boot camp was both physically and mentally demanding, but I pushed through. The hardest part? There was no smoking and no drinking. It was the first time since I was 13 that I had gone without alcohol. Surprisingly, I didn't have any withdrawals, and I managed to make it through.

While in boot camp, Melissa wrote me letters, which gave me something to look forward to. When I graduated, I was transferred to Dam Neck, Virginia, where I enrolled in radar school for three months. That's when Melissa joined me, and we married in Virginia Beach.

After finishing radar school, I was assigned to the Naval Air Station in Norfolk, Virginia, where I finally boarded my ship—the U.S.S. Truett (FF-1095). That's when my real life as a shipboard sailor began.

Chapter 3
Dear John

The moment I stepped onto my ship, the excitement was overwhelming. I had spent five long months training for this—five months of learning, preparing, and envisioning what life would be like aboard a warship in the formidable 6th Fleet. And now, finally, I had arrived.

I was officially a radar man, though my title on paper was "Operations Specialist." The weight of my responsibilities hit me immediately. Our ship's primary mission was clear: track Soviet submarines, document their movements, and pinpoint their locations with unwavering precision. The Cold War was at its peak, and every blip on the radar could mean something significant. We were the eyes in the dark, the silent watchers of the sea.

But before I could step into my role, I had to go through the time-honored tradition that awaited every new arrival: 90 days of washing dishes. It was the unspoken rule, the rite of passage, the humbling initiation that no one was exempt from.

I had envisioned something more grandiose, something befitting the prestige of serving on a warship. Yet, there I was, standing in front of a mountain of dirty dishes, back to my very first job—dishwashing. The sting of reality was sharp, but I refused to let it dull my enthusiasm. It was a humble job, and I embraced it.

I made friends, and in those three months, we found ways to laugh and make the best of our situation.

Life outside the ship was a stark contrast. Melissa and I had an apartment off-base, a little sanctuary away from the chaos of military life. When my ship was in port, it almost felt like I was working a normal nine-to-five job. I would come home to a warm meal, a loving wife, and the quiet comforts of civilian life. It was a rhythm I could get used to.

But the military isn't built for comfort. Orders came down—we were deploying to the Mediterranean Sea. This was it, my first real deployment. It also meant my first extended separation from Melissa since basic training. As we pulled away from Norfolk, Virginia, I could feel the weight of it. The open ocean stretched before us, and with it, the unknown.

As the weeks at sea turned into months, I noticed a trend among my shipmates. 'Dear John' letters began arriving— breakup letters from wives and girlfriends who couldn't handle the distance, the loneliness, the uncertainty. I watched tough men crumble under the weight of those words. I prayed I wouldn't be next.

But prayers don't always change fate. When my turn came, I stared at the letter in my hands, my heart pounding as I read the words that shattered the life I had envisioned. Melissa had moved on. In hindsight, I should have known. We were both young, from a small town, and the military world was foreign to us. I had left her in a place filled with single sailors, and reality had taken its course.

I had two choices—let it break me, or push forward. I chose the latter. I buried the pain and threw myself into the distractions of military life.

Our ship made several Ports of Call across Europe, brief respites in the grind of deployment. Italy, Spain, France—each stop is an adventure of its own. For young sailors like us, these ports were a dream, designed to cater to our kind. Wine, women, and song—temptations at every turn.

I found solace in friendship, in the camaraderie of those who understood what I was going through. My best friend on the ship was Mike from Tennessee. We had similar upbringings, and in the chaos of military life, we had each other's backs. That bond lasted beyond deployment, beyond years, beyond distance. To this day, Mike remains one of my closest friends.

During this time, I finally completed my 90-day dishwashing assignment and took my place in the combat information center. My job? Manning is a surface radar. It was a different world—dark, air-conditioned, the glow of the radar screens casting eerie reflections across the room. Here, we tracked, we monitored, and we anticipated. My chief, Chief Mundt, was a no-nonsense man. Stern, unyielding, the kind of leader who made sure you never got too comfortable. Under his watch, I became sharper, more disciplined, and attuned to the precision my job demanded.

After six months, we returned to Norfolk. The ship went into dry dock for maintenance and repairs, marking a temporary pause in the relentless cycle of deployment. By then, the inevitable had happened—Melissa and I were officially divorced. There was nothing left to salvage, nothing to hold on to.

For the next year, as the ship underwent its necessary repairs, my buddies and I embraced the freedom that came with it. We had no immediate deployments, no impending orders—just time, time to let loose, time to reclaim a part of ourselves that the Navy hadn't yet molded. We were young, single, and in the prime of our lives, and for that moment, we lived like we were invincible.

Chapter 4
Wine, Women, and Song

During my time in the Navy, I formed a close-knit group consisting of four of us—my best friend Mike, Tim from Georgia, and John from Michigan—along with myself. We were all sailors stationed on the same ship, and our bond quickly grew into a brotherhood.

John happened to own a van, which we affectionately nicknamed 'The Mobile Assault Vehicle'. This van became more than just a mode of transportation; it was our headquarters, our sanctuary, and our means of adventure. The four of us considered ourselves its crew, always ready for the next escapade.

At that stage in our lives, we were all young, single, and eager to make the most of our time ashore. Our primary mission was simple—hit as many bars as possible and embrace everything that came with it: Wine, Women, and Song. We would drive the van from one bar to another, meeting women, drinking, and indulging in the reckless freedom of youth.

Our nights were wild and filled with endless fun. We partied, danced, and enjoyed the carefree lifestyle that came with being young sailors on leave. Among the many spots we frequented, two stood out—Knickerbockers and The Brass Rail. These bars had a reputation, but what shocked me the most was a strange pattern I noticed. More than once, I danced with a woman only for her to reveal that her husband was about to be deployed. Without hesitation, she would suggest that I move in with her. This happened to me three or four times, and I found it absolutely mind-blowing. I had never encountered anything like it before.

Though I never accepted any of those offers, I appreciated knowing that I had a place to go when I wasn't on the ship. That all changed one night when I found myself in a situation that made me rethink everything.

I was at a woman's house, casually sitting in her living room, wearing her husband's bathrobe. Then, out of nowhere, the phone rang. It was her husband, calling from Beirut, Lebanon. At that moment, a wave of guilt hit me. I could hear the love and longing in his voice as he spoke to his wife from a war zone, and it struck a nerve. I had been deployed before—I knew what it was like to be away, worrying about home. It was in that instant that I realized what I was doing was wrong. I couldn't continue down that path, so I decided to stop.

Despite the chaos of our nightlife, we somehow managed to make it back to the ship in the mornings, a feat we called 'The Morning Miracle'. After a full night of drinking and bar-hopping, it was nothing short of miraculous that we not only made it back on time for muster but also managed to be in full uniform and somewhat presentable.

Beyond the bars, we sought out other forms of entertainment as well. We attended concerts and took road trips back to our hometowns whenever we had the chance. It was during this time that I reconnected with my cousin, Margie, who lived in Norfolk. In 1984, she introduced me to her friend Erin.

At the time, I had no idea that Erin would go on to become my second wife and the mother of my two children. But before that, she became an honorary member of The Mobile Assault Crew. She embraced the lifestyle and joined right in with our debauchery. Over time, however, something changed. Erin and I grew closer, and what started as a wild and carefree fling turned into something deeper.

As the months passed, our relationship became more exclusive, and the reckless adventures of The Mobile Assault Crew slowly faded into the background. This chapter of my life came to a close in 1985 when I was honorably discharged from the Navy, marking the end of an era and the beginning of something new.

Chapter 5
Drifting, Detours, and Destiny

After my discharge from the Navy, I didn't exactly have a master plan. Scratch that—I didn't have any plan at all. I was floating aimlessly, trying to figure out my next move, when my girlfriend, Erin, mentioned that her sister lived in Raleigh, North Carolina. Well, that was more of a plan than I had at the time, so why not? We packed up whatever we owned—which wasn't much—stuffed it into our car, and set off for North Carolina like a couple of wide-eyed wanderers chasing an uncertain future.

Once we arrived, we rented a small apartment and attempted to piece together something resembling an adult life. Erin managed to land an office job, while I found work in a warehouse. And by "work," I mean a series of dead-end jobs that amounted to nothing more than sore muscles and an ever-growing sense of dissatisfaction. Life was painfully uneventful, a dull routine of work, sleep, repeat. But, as life tends to do, it

threw us a curveball—Erin got pregnant.

This was 1985, and suddenly, the stakes were much higher. Neither of us had much money, nor did we have a solid support system in North Carolina. That realization hit me like a freight train, so I made the decision to move back to Huntington, West Virginia, where my family lived. Maybe, just maybe, they could help us get on our feet.

Our financial situation was so bleak that renting a U-Haul was a luxury beyond our means. Instead, we did what any desperate and slightly ridiculous young couple would do—we loaded all of our worldly possessions into a wooden boat and used it as our makeshift moving van. It was hardly the picture of stability, but it got the job done.

When we arrived at my mother's house, she took us in without hesitation. For the first time in a while, I felt a little less lost. She was an incredible help, allowing us to stay for a month or two while we scraped together enough money to rent our own place. Erin managed to find another clerical job, and I, in an act of pure entrepreneurial desperation, decided to start buying and selling used cars.

The plan was simple: I'd go to car auctions in Kentucky, buy a couple of cheap, questionable vehicles, and pray they survived the trip back home. Sometimes, I got lucky. Other times, not so much. But I cleaned them up and sold them for as much profit as I could squeeze out. It wasn't glamorous, but it kept the lights on. During this time, I also decided to enroll at Marshall University for a semester, taking general education classes. It was the first time in a long while that I felt like I was doing something productive, something that actually improved me as a person.

Then, in 1986, my daughter was born. The moment she came into this world, everything changed. I was ecstatic but also terrified. One amazing coincidence is that my daughter was born in the same hospital and room as her mother, Erin. And Erin never mentioned to me that she was born here in West Virginia. How were we going to support a baby when we were barely keeping our heads above water? The financial strain was a constant weight on my shoulders, and I knew we had to figure something out—fast.

Erin had mentioned her father in passing a few times, casually dropping tidbits about how he lived in New Orleans, Louisiana. That little detail suddenly seemed important. I had made it clear to Erin when we first moved to West Virginia that she shouldn't put down roots here. The place was drowning in poverty and had little to offer in terms of

opportunity. Then, one day, her father called. Erin handed me the phone, and before I knew it, one conversation led to another, and—well—I may have invited us to New Orleans without really asking first.

I was beyond thrilled. This was our shot at a fresh start, a chance to build something better for our daughter. We said our goodbyes, packed up our belongings—this time, we could actually afford a U-Haul—and braced ourselves for the next chapter. We drove 18 hours straight to New Orleans with a baby in tow, fueled by a desperate hope that life would be kinder to us there.

Only time would tell if we had made the right decision.

Chapter 6
The Big Easy

Arriving in New Orleans was like stepping into an entirely different world. I had never seen a city so alive, so rich with culture and history, and yet so unfamiliar. It was a huge cultural shock for me. The streets buzzed with energy, a mix of old and new, where jazz played from hidden corners and the scent of Creole cuisine filled the air. The city, mostly Black with a strong French Creole influence, was unlike anything I had ever experienced. Erin felt the same way—overwhelmed, yet intrigued by the place her father called home.

Her father was an upper-middle-class man, a pilot guiding ships along the Mississippi River. When we arrived at his house, I quickly picked up on the tension between him and Erin. He was distant, his demeanor cold, and I sensed a strained relationship between them. I imagined their past, how the relationship between him and Erin's mother had crumbled, leaving Erin longing for a connection that he seemed reluctant to give. She wanted to be close to him, to rebuild something from the broken pieces, but he kept his walls up, almost as if he was trying to make up for lost time without fully committing to it.

Despite his distant nature, he got me a job on the Mississippi River. It was hard, dangerous work. My role was to dock ships that came from all over the world. Massive ropes and thick wire ties had to be dragged and secured to keep the ships steady. Sometimes, we took small boats into the river to secure tie lines to buoys, battling the powerful currents that never rested. The job didn't stop for the weather—whether it was dark, raining, or the winds howled, we had to be out there. I was paid an average wage and worked grueling 24-hour shifts. Occasionally, I found moments of rest in a van between dockings, but the exhaustion never fully left my bones.

Meanwhile, Erin found a clerical job at an office. We managed to get an apartment together, and our little girl, Jennifer, went to daycare while we worked to make ends meet. Though we were trying to settle, I faced another challenge at work. I was an outsider among the men on the docks—most were born and raised in New Orleans, and I was just some guy trying to fit in. I did my best, keeping my head down and proving myself through hard work.

In 1988, life shifted again—Erin became pregnant. We welcomed our son, Justin, into the world that year. Having two kids made things even more stressful, especially since we weren't making much money. But in the midst of our struggles, we embraced the culture around us. We became part of the rhythm of New Orleans.

We went to the Mardi Gras parades, massive events that saw up to a million people in the streets. The parades had celebrity grand marshals, wild floats, and beads flying through the air. Some women would expose their boobs for trinkets, while others caught them with laughter and joy. It was a family event with an unmistakable air of indulgence and extravagance.

With two children, marriage felt inevitable. In 1989, we made it official, signing papers in front of the Justice of the Peace. No grand wedding, no fanfare—just a simple legal ceremony that made us husband and wife on paper.

But soon after, something changed between us. Tension grew. Alcohol became a factor. We both drank, but I drank a little more, and it started creating cracks in our fragile foundation. Erin wasn't happy, and I could feel the distance forming between us. Eventually, I moved out and went to stay with my buddy, Eddie.

For about eight or nine months, I lived in a fish camp on Lake Pontchartrain. I was single again, and Eddie and I partied our way through the French Quarter. The bars never closed—some didn't even have doors, having been open since the day they started. Bourbon Street was a playground of indulgence, filled with people looking to escape their realities.

Despite my new lifestyle, part of me still longed for Erin. I didn't want the separation, and it hurt more than I let on. Occasionally, we would spend days together, attempting to fix what was broken. But the final nail in the coffin came the day I visited her apartment and noticed the carpet burns on her back—marks left by another man. I didn't need to ask. The realization cut deep. The relationship was over.

New Orleans started to weigh on me. The partying, the drinking, the city itself—it was all too much. I needed a change. By that time, my family had moved to St. Petersburg, Florida. In 1990, I packed up everything I owned into my Volkswagen camper van, took my five-year-old daughter, Jennifer, and left The Big Easy behind.

As I drove away, the city disappeared in my rearview mirror, but its imprint on my life remained. It had given me memories, love, loss, and a son I would always cherish. But it had also given me lessons—some painful, some eye-opening. With Jennifer beside me, we headed toward a new beginning in St. Petersburg, Florida, leaving behind the echoes of a past that had run its course.

Chapter 7
Sunshine, Sand, and Shifts

Saint Petersburg, Florida. A new city. A new chapter. Me My daughter and I arrived with only a few bags and a suitcase full of hope. The salty air felt foreign to my lungs, and the blazing Florida sun glared down like it was daring me to find my place beneath it. But through the haze of uncertainty and sweat, there she was — my mom, arms wide open, heart full of the same unwavering support that had carried me through too many storms already.

There was my mom helping again. Like clockwork. No lectures, no judgment — just space, warmth, and that quiet strength only a mother can bring. Her house became our safe landing, a pause between turbulence and whatever came next.

The Florida lifestyle, though, was another major adjustment. It was like stepping into another world entirely. I had never seen beaches like these in my life, endless white sand, waves that whispered secrets to the shore, and people living like tomorrow didn't matter. Scantily clad women walked around like the beach was their runway and the party. It was always on. Day or night, it pulsed through the city like a living thing, pulling people into its rhythm.

But I had my daughter with me. And that one fact tempered everything. I couldn't let myself get swept away, no matter how tempting. I behaved, at least to a degree. My wild side curled itself up somewhere deep inside, replaced by the reality of parenthood and responsibility.

That reality hit harder when the money started running out, and I knew I had to find work. Quickly. But finding something stable wasn't as easy as I hoped. I ended up signing on with a temp agency, and what followed was one of the most humbling experiences of my life. They sent me to job after job, most of it unskilled labor. Nothing glamorous. Nothing permanent.

The pay? $5.25 an hour. I was shocked. The difference in pay between New Orleans and Florida slapped me hard. It wasn't just the money, it was the blow to my pride. I had worked real jobs before. Now I was just another name on a list, shuffled from one factory floor to another. One week, they sent me to GTE, the company that printed the Yellow Pages.

The noise, the machines, the smell of ink and paper — it all felt heavy. And so did the fear. I didn't want to be stuck in this cycle, floating from one temporary job to the next like a ghost with no address. So one day, I asked someone where the plant manager's office was.

I don't know what came over me, but I made my way there, heart pounding. I knocked on the door.

"Come in," he said, without looking up.

I stepped inside and introduced myself.

"Sir, my name is Jim," I began. I handed him my resume — clean, professional, printed on decent paper — and told him the truth. That I'd never worked for a temp agency before. That I wasn't just looking for a paycheck. I was looking for a job. A real one. With benefits. With dignity. With a future.

He looked it over. Asked a few questions. And that was that, or so I thought.

The very next day, he called me back into his office. Offered me a job. A proper job. I was to work in the printing plant. It wasn't glamorous, far from it. But it was something solid. Something mine. And that mattered.

Around this time, my ex-wife started visiting Saint Petersburg with my son. Part of it, I think, was for her to see our daughter. But the other part, maybe just as important, was for me to see my boy. For those few hours, our fractured family would find a strange kind of rhythm again, like pieces of a song that still managed to harmonize, if only briefly.

Then one visit changed everything.

She sat across from me, calm, almost too calm. She told me she had met someone, a man from Australia. I didn't think much of it at the time. People meet people. It's what we do. But that meeting would become the catalyst for a profound shift in my life. I just didn't know it yet.

And so Saint Petersburg became a strange intersection of endings and beginnings, sunshine and hard labor, of old wounds and new chapters. I came here searching for stability. What I found was transformation.

Chapter 8
The Long Silence and the Song

When Erin asked to take Jennifer to New Orleans for a while, I agreed. Maybe I was trying to keep the peace. Maybe I believed that temporary distance might heal the wounds still fresh between us. Looking back, I see now that it was one of the worst mistakes of my life.

A week or two passed. Quiet crept in slowly, like a fog you don't notice until you're lost in it. I hadn't heard from my kids. No phone calls. No messages. Just silence. At first, I told myself not to panic. But the father in me knew something wasn't right.

So I started calling, reaching out, checking in, and making inquiries. And that's when it hit me like a freight train: every single number I dialed had been disconnected. Every line is gone.

I called my old friend Eddie in New Orleans. He owed me a few favors, so I asked him to go by the apartment. When he finally called me back, his voice was low and heavy: the place was empty. Completely vacated.

Erin, the custodial parent, had vanished. She had violated the court orders and disappeared without a trace. Somewhere deep in my gut, I knew what had happened. I suspected she'd taken the kids to Australia with her new boyfriend. The thought swallowed me whole.

And this was before the internet. No Facebook, no email, no easy search tools. I was a father armed with nothing but a disconnected phone line and desperation. I tried the New Orleans police. I called them repeatedly. Begged them. But all they said was, "It's a civil matter."

I clung to hope—maybe she'd call. Maybe she'd let me talk to them, tell them I loved them. But she never did. Days turned to months. Months into years. Twelve of them.

Twelve long years.

And when I did finally see them again… they were grown. Strangers with British accents. My babies—foreign to my ears and unfamiliar in their eyes.

Somewhere in that lost time, my paternal grandparents passed away. It was at their funeral that I was finally allowed to go through some of my father's personal effects—the same father who had been murdered so many years before.

In his belongings, I found his wallet. I held it in my hands like a fragile relic from a forgotten life. Inside were the expected things: his driver's license and some old receipts. But then, something unexpected—a small, carefully folded piece of paper.

It was a spelling test. One of mine. A perfect score in bold red ink.

He had carried it with him. All those years. I stood there, stunned. My father had been proud of me. Even after all that time, he had carried proof of my small victory close to his heart. That discovery lit a quiet, warm flame in the dark place

I had lived in for so long. He was gone, but he had believed in me. He had loved me.

Back then, I had been working nights in Saint Petersburg, Florida, third shift at the Saint Petersburg Times. It was better than the factory work I'd done before, but still soul-draining. Sleep-deprived and barely making ends meet. But it gave me just enough to finally buy my first home. That meant something.

One night, my brother John took me to a bar. Just to get out of the house, maybe chase a little laughter. That's where I first saw karaoke. The place was alive—laughter, beer, voices echoing over tinny backing tracks. I was hooked.

I talked to the guy running it, got some advice, then bought my own karaoke system. I slapped my name on a stack of business cards. Suddenly, I was in business, hosting shows on the side while still working nights at the Times.

The karaoke world was wild. Electric. I met so many people—so many characters. Some you couldn't invent if you tried. One man came to every single show dressed as Elvis Presley. His outfit looked like it had been rescued from a thrift store fire. Every time, he'd pull me aside—serious as a heart attack—and ask me to introduce him as Walter Cash, Johnny Cash's brother.

While dressed like Elvis.

He did it every week, and each time, you'd think it was his first time asking. He couldn't carry a tune to save his life, which somehow made his act even more unforgettable. The comedy of it all never faded.

And then one night, everything changed.

I was out driving and pulled into a carnival. I wasn't expecting much—just a little distraction. But as I wandered through the lights and the music, I came across a girl working one of the pool games. She had the kind of smile that could slow time. Her name was Sandra.

She was absolutely beautiful. There was a spark between us—instant and undeniable. I was hooked.

What I didn't know then was how life-changing that moment would be.

Chapter 9
The Joy and The Reckoning

When Sandra and I met, it was as if sparks flew instantly. There was no hesitation—we dove into a relationship immediately and moved in together without second-guessing it. We found a cozy little apartment and quickly settled into a rhythm that, for a while, felt like the carefree life we both needed.

Our days were filled with laughter and adventure. We'd spend long afternoons at the beach, toes in the sand, soaking in the sun and each other. Nights were made for parties, karaoke, and the kind of wild fun that made us feel young and untouchable. Our involvement in the karaoke business blurred the lines between work and play, and honestly, there was a lot more partying than business. But we didn't mind. At that moment in time, it all felt right.

When I first met Sandra, she told me she was unable to have children. I took that in stride—it didn't change how I felt about her. I accepted it wholeheartedly, never imagining anything different. But then, seemingly out of nowhere, she told me she was pregnant.

To say I was surprised would be an understatement. Shocked might be more accurate. It changed everything. The days of constant parties and carefree indulgence were behind us. Life had taken a sharp turn, and it was time to grow up. I was going to be a father. I wanted to be a good one.

But before I had time to adjust to this new reality, another one came knocking—literally.

It was during Sandra's pregnancy that a sheriff's deputy showed up at our door. He asked if I was Jim Hammonds. I nodded, a little confused, and he handed me a thick envelope—legal documents. I tore into them, heart pounding, and read words that stopped me cold: paternity papers for a thirteen-year-old girl named Rachael.

I was blindsided. I sat down, papers trembling in my hands, trying to make sense of it. As I flipped through the documents, one name jumped out at me. It stirred a faint memory—something buried deep. I suddenly recalled a one-time encounter I'd had years ago while visiting my grandparents. I'd met a girl, sweet and soft-spoken, who had told me she was a virgin. I believed her. What I didn't know—what I couldn't have imagined—was that night would lead to a life I wouldn't learn about until more than a decade later.

I had never heard from her again. No letters. No phone calls. No whispers. Nothing. And now, I was being told I had a daughter.

I reached out to Rachael. We started talking on the phone, slowly, carefully. Eventually, I invited her to come visit me in St. Petersburg. When she arrived, it was…awkward. There was no bond to speak of, no shared memories to cling to. We were strangers bound by blood, trying to figure out what that meant. Over time, Rachael went on to have two beautiful children of her own, and though we stayed in touch, our relationship never quite blossomed. There was always a strange distance between us. I was never really a dad to her—not the way I wished I could've been. But that wasn't her fault. Life just…happened the way it did.

In 1992, Sandra gave birth to our son, Dakoda. Holding him in my arms for the first time filled a space in my heart I didn't know was empty. I was overwhelmed with joy. He was my world. Being a father to him was a blessing I treasured.

But even in the midst of that joy, a darker cloud loomed. Sandra and I were drinking too much. The fun had turned into a crutch, and it was affecting everything. I knew something had to change—not just for me, but for Dakoda. He deserved better.

So I did the hardest thing I've ever done—I raised my hand and admitted I had a problem. I enrolled in my employer's Substance Abuse Program and checked into rehab. I asked Sandra to come with me, hoping we could change together. But she wasn't ready. She loved the lifestyle too much to let it go. So she made her choice and walked away from me, and from Dakoda.

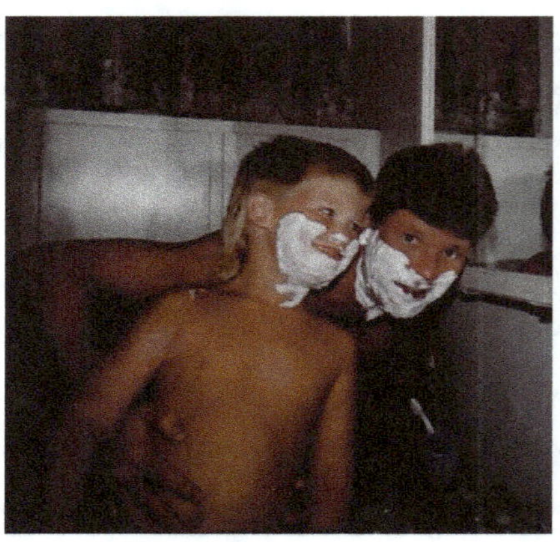

It was heartbreaking, but I couldn't let that stop me. I hired a lawyer, fought for custody, and was granted full guardianship of my son. My mother—my rock—stepped in once again, just like she always did. She cared for Dakoda while I was in treatment, and her unwavering support held me steady. I've never had a better friend than my mom. Her strength carried me when mine was running thin.

After just eight days, I came out of rehab and walked straight into the rooms of Alcoholics Anonymous. That's where my real journey began. I committed myself to sobriety—not just for me, but for my son. Raising Dakoda as a single father became my purpose, my pride, my joy.

It wasn't the path I imagined, but it was the one that saved me. And for that, I'm forever grateful.

Chapter 10
The Shift

It was around this time that restlessness started to gnaw at me. I had spent too many nights under the mechanical hum of the press machines at The Times. The job was loud, the air thick with ink and dust, and the third shift never allowed for much daylight. It was the kind of work that aged you from the inside out — repetitive, unremarkable, and draining. I knew I needed out. Not just from that job, but from the version of myself it had caged.

A friend of mine suggested I check out Terminex, a pest control company. The idea felt random at first — pest control? — But anything that promised a cleaner, quieter future was worth a shot. I scheduled an appointment with the branch manager for an interview, not knowing that this meeting would set off a chain of events that would change my life.

I went in expecting to be considered for a technician's role — boots-on-the-ground, eradicating bugs, something tangible I could do with my hands. But after talking to me for a while, the manager leaned forward, eyes sharp, and said, "Have you ever thought about sales?"

Sales? That wasn't what I came for. But something in his tone, a confidence I didn't yet have in myself, made me say yes. That "yes" turned out to be one of the best decisions I ever made.

After just a brief training period, I became the number one salesman in the branch during my first month. It felt surreal. I had spent my life doing blue-collar work — work that left me dirty, tired, and invisible. But now, I was dressing in clean, sharp clothes, shaking hands with homeowners in the suburbs, and closing deals like a seasoned pro.

Something awakened in me. I had a gift I never knew existed — the ability to connect with strangers, to earn their trust and their business. Each visit became a game, a challenge. I'd walk into a stranger's home by appointment, explain what we did, and walk out with a signed contract and a check or credit card. And I loved it.

For the first time, I was making real money. The kind of money that lets you breathe. The bosses noticed, too. I was being taken to lunch, handed bonuses, and treated like I mattered. This was a world away from the factory floors of my past.

Soon, I was buying cars, investing, saving, and even buying my first house. I was building a new life — one that felt like it had direction, dignity, and color.

On weekends, I picked up a part-time job as a bouncer at a local nightclub. It wasn't for the money — I did it for fun, for the buzz of it. There was a lot of action at the bar, and it was a great place to meet women. And that's where I met Denise.

She was a beautiful redhead, radiant and full of energy. She had a little girl who was about the same age as my son. We hit it off quickly, and before long, she moved in with me. Denise had a warm, domestic touch. She'd cook amazing meals, clean the house, and take care of everything. She drank socially, while I remained sober at the time.

But even with everything in place — the job, the money, the companionship — my heart was restless. Something in me was still searching. After a year, the relationship ended. It was mutual. We stayed friends, and I never knew her to have touched drugs.

Years later, I got the call — Denise had died of an overdose.

The news hit me like a fist to the chest. I stood in disbelief at her funeral, surrounded by photos, my photos of her, displayed on the tables, images of a life that had once briefly intertwined with mine. I mourned her, not just for what she became, but for what she had once been.

Life moved on. I kept selling pest control by day and bouncing at the bar by night. That's when I met Shonna, the "shooter girl" at the club. She was stunning — long blonde hair, built like a dream, and, more importantly, sober. No alcohol. No drugs. I was drawn to her instantly. That attraction would grow into love, and I would eventually marry this woman.

But while my personal life was blooming again, tragedy struck my family.

My younger brother John was in a horrific motorcycle accident. He was rushed to Bay Front Hospital and taken straight into the ICU. The doctors told us he had a severe head injury and only a ten percent chance of surviving.

Our entire family gathered in the waiting room, and let me tell you something — you don't see atheists in an ICU waiting room. When life hangs by a thread, even the strongest skeptics whisper to God.

My mother and I never left the hospital. I juggled hospital visits between my sales appointments, just trying to be near him, to believe in him. John, even though he was younger than I, was always the tough one. When we were growing up, he looked out for me and our brother David. He was fearless. Protective. Solid.

Watching him in that hospital bed was unbearable. But against all odds — defying science, logic, and every grim prognosis — he pulled through.

He lived.

And today, he's not just my brother. He's my best friend.

That season of my life was a whirlwind, full of transformation, love, loss, and miracles. I discovered what I was capable of. I climbed out of the grime of factory life and into a version of myself I could be proud of. I learned how fragile and precious life is, how quickly it can be stolen away, and how powerful the human spirit can be when it chooses to fight.

This chapter of my life wasn't just about changing jobs.

It was about changing me.

Chapter 11
Echoes of the Past

After twelve long years of silence, a voice from another lifetime found its way back to me. Erin, my ex-wife, the woman who had once absconded with our children, was on the other end of the line. I froze. I hadn't heard her voice in over a decade, and it stirred something deep, something long buried. Shock coursed through me, not because I was angry, though there was plenty of reason to be, but because I had long since given up hope of ever hearing anything about my kids. I didn't know if they were alive or dead. The silence had been that complete.

She had remarried, she told me. An Australian man. They had three children together. I was surprised, not at the marriage itself, but at the fact that she had built an entirely new life while erasing our old one. Now, she explained, her marriage was unraveling, and she felt like an outcast in her Australian community. There was a crack in her voice as she apologized, but to be honest, I didn't care much for her excuses or explanations. I didn't need idle chit-chat. I just wanted to see my children.

We agreed to meet in Florida. For the first time in twelve years, I would lay eyes on my son and daughter. But just before the trip, I discovered Erin had invited herself along. The kids were 16 and 18, more than old enough to travel alone, and frankly, they didn't want her there either. Still, she insisted, and I had to accept it. There was no alternative.

Unlike my daughter Rachael, whom I had never had the chance to bond with, these two weren't strangers. I had lived with them, laughed with them, loved them. They were once my everything. I picked them up from the airport and brought them back to my place in Florida, where my son Dakoda—my only child from another relationship—was waiting. He was curious and excited; for the first time, he was meeting the siblings he never knew he had. He'd grown up believing he was an only child.

Around that time, my relationship with Shonna, whom we often jokingly referred to as the "shooter girl," came to its inevitable end. It had always been tempestuous. Once she moved into my home, everything began to crumble. She was obsessed with my will, constantly pestering me about whether she was included in it. It became a running joke among my friends and family, her fixation bordering on comical, if not uncomfortable. The more I avoided the topic, the more obsessed she became. For the record, she was never in my will. Eventually, we ended things amicably. We remained friends. That's always been my way. You never know when you'll need to cross a bridge again.

My ex, Shonna, had this installed not long before we broke up.

Back to my children, what a surreal experience it was. Both spoke with thick British accents. It was jarring at first. I had never heard them speak like that. My son seemed like your average teenage boy, guarded yet curious. But my daughter Jennifer… she was different. I could sense a quiet pain beneath the surface. Justin, my son, was too young when Erin took them to remember our life together. But Jennifer had memories, vivid ones. And Erin had done her best to erase them.

I later learned that Erin had forbidden them from mentioning my name in their new household. No photos. No stories. No memories. That kind of erasure is a form of psychological abuse. A child deserves their full history, not a curated one.

Despite the awkward beginnings, our time together in Florida was beautiful. We laughed, reconnected, and began building a new bridge from the ruins of the old one. After they returned to Australia, we kept in touch. Justin and I grew close, he's visited the ranch several times since. He married a lovely woman named Charlotte, and they now have a baby girl, Talia. They are a cherished part of my family, and I count myself blessed every day for having them in my life.

Jennifer, though, remains a more complex story. Her journey hasn't been easy. I suspect that, in the absence of her father and the trauma of being taken away so young, she turned to substances to numb the pain. She's currently in a rehabilitation program and appears to be doing well. She has two beautiful sons, and we're a work in progress. She's brilliant and beautiful, and there is no reason she can't live a happy, fulfilled life if she's willing to put in the work.

During this time, another emotional wave hit our family. We received a call from North Carolina, Sandra's mother. Sandra, Dakoda's mom, was gravely ill. Her liver had all but failed from years of drinking. She was in hospice care at home, and her mother urged us to come immediately if we wanted to see her again.

It shook me. I had heard murmurs of her struggles, but nothing had prepared me for the sight I saw when we arrived. Sandra lay frail and fading in her mother's house. Despite everything that had transpired between us, there was no bitterness. She was still the mother of my son. We talked and shared memories, and she thanked me—sincerely—for raising Dakoda. I could see how hard it was on him. They hadn't been close, and he hadn't seen much of her since she moved away, but there's a hole only a mother can fill. And I know that pain intimately. As we laid her on her deathbed, I knew I would never see her alive again. It made me sad.

I gave them time alone to talk, to say the things they needed to say. Then we returned to Florida.

Three weeks later, she passed.

Life has a way of bringing everything full circle. Some stories end with closure, others with quiet sorrow. But through all of it, love and connection endure. And so, I move forward—rebuilding what was broken, embracing the family I have, and hoping that, no matter the time or distance, healing will always find its way through.

Chapter 12
A Door Knock Into the Wild

One day at work, life took an unexpected turn.

I was working as a pest control consultant, and on this particular day, my office sent me to a client's house in St. Petersburg. It seemed like any other assignment, routine, and uneventful. I had no idea that this random appointment would end up changing the course of my life.

As I approached the house, everything appeared completely normal. Nothing stood out, just a quiet residential street and a well-kept home like any other. Nothing about it suggested anything out of the ordinary.

I knocked on the door, and a customer opened it with a polite nod, welcoming me inside.

We began chatting about their pest control concerns, just like I had done with dozens of other clients before. I asked the usual questions, and they described a few areas in the house where they had noticed signs of trouble. With my equipment in hand, I started to inspect the home thoroughly for any pest-related problems.

As I moved through the house, I caught something out of the corner of my eye, a sudden, small movement. I assumed it was a cat or some small household pet, nothing unusual.

But then I turned to take a better look.

What I saw made me freeze in my tracks.

It wasn't a cat.

It was a monkey. A ring-tailed lemur, to be exact.

I was startled, a mix of shock and pure curiosity swept over me. I stood there, momentarily speechless. I'd never been this close to a lemur before, only from behind the glass at the zoo.

And there it was, right in front of me.

As I observed the lemur in fascination, I noticed two more tiny figures nearby, two baby lemurs, crawling close by and peeking out from behind furniture.

I must have looked completely enchanted because the customer caught on and smiled. Perhaps sensing my amazement, they casually said something I didn't expect:

"If you're interested in the babies, we'll give you a great deal."

It had never occurred to me, not even once, to buy a monkey. It wasn't something I was planning, or even dreaming of. But at that moment, something just clicked. Whether it was impulse or intuition, I heard myself say:

"I'll take them."

The very next day, the customer showed up at my house with the two baby lemurs.

My son Dakoda and I were beyond excited. We couldn't stop smiling as we brought them into our home. That same day, we quickly got to work and constructed an enclosure in our garage, making sure it was safe, secure, and cozy for the new arrivals.

These lemurs had been tamed as pets, but since they were parent-raised, they didn't enjoy being picked up. Still, they were gentle and social, they would crawl all over us, leaping from shoulder to shoulder, and clinging to us with their soft, curious hands.

We were completely fascinated. Every little sound they made, every little behavior felt magical.

As days went by, we'd often leave our garage door open, and the presence of the lemurs began catching the attention of others. Neighbors stopped in their tracks. Passersby peeked in with wide eyes. Kids would run up to get a glimpse, and even adults couldn't hide their surprise.

Everyone who saw them reacted the same way, drawn in, amazed.

That's when I began to notice just how much people were gravitating toward these exotic animals. They sparked something in everyone, wonder, joy, curiosity.

It got me thinking.

I started spending time online, researching the exotic animal trade. I dove into articles, forums, videos—anything I could get my hands on. I read stories, watched firsthand experiences, and explored the realities of owning and caring for exotic pets.

There were both negative and positive sides to it, and I paid attention to both. I knew it wasn't something to take lightly.

But what stuck with me most was how much attention these animals brought. It wasn't just curiosity, it was a connection.

That's when I seriously began considering it as a potential business opportunity.

I focused my efforts and began gathering information on primates in the pet trade. I learned about different species, care routines, breeding ethics, and more.

Florida, luckily, was awash in monkeys. The state's climate, laws, and existing breeders made it a hot spot for this kind of trade.

From everything I found, one species stood out to me: the common marmoset. They were small, expressive, popular, and more affordable than many other primates. They seemed to be the ideal breed for first-time monkey owners.

So I started thinking more seriously about buying adult marmosets, breeding them, and selling the babies myself.

To take the next step, I applied for and obtained a breeder's license from the state of Florida. It was official.

Thankfully, I was in a good place financially. My pest control business had been doing well, and I knew this wasn't a cheap endeavor. Everything, from enclosures to health checkups, had to be done properly.

You can't get into this business on the cheap.

But despite doing everything right, I hit a major wall early on.

In my research and outreach, I quickly discovered that about 99% of the contacts I made were scammers. Fake listings. Shady sellers. Too-good-to-be-true offers. It was overwhelming.

But I kept going. I refused to give up.

Eventually, I found my way through. Through the chaos and false leads, I came across someone real—someone knowledgeable and trustworthy.

From this point forward, they will be known as the 'Marmoset Queen.'

And that's where a new chapter in my life truly began.

51

Chapter 13
The Marmoset Queen

It all started with a trip I had arranged to visit a man I mockingly called "The Marmoset Queen." The nickname came to me almost instinctively. There was something about the way he presented himself online, like he ruled the kingdom of exotic animals with a jeweled crown and a velvet robe. I was planning to buy Marmosets from him. This was my very first real interaction with someone directly involved in the exotic animal business.

I remember being both excited and nervous. I had no experience, none. But I was eager to learn, eager to step into this fascinating world I had only seen from afar.

When my girlfriend and I arrived at his property, reality slapped us square in the face. What greeted us wasn't the grandeur I'd imagined from his confident online persona, it was chaos. Dozens of boxes filled with rotting produce were scattered outside, each one cloaked in a thick, buzzing cloud of flies.

We stepped out of the car, hesitating. I turned to her and raised an eyebrow. She didn't say anything, but her eyes narrowed, mirroring my concern.

"This isn't exactly what I expected," I muttered.

She replied dryly, "You sure this isn't a landfill tour?"

We were invited inside the house, and if we thought the outside was bad, we were in for a shock.

Inside, the place was overrun with small animals crammed into tiny cages, reptiles, birds, mammals, you name it. It was less of a home and more of a living, breathing, chaotic petting zoo. The smell hit us next. A heavy, sour mixture of urine, feces, and decay lingered thick in the air.

"Lovely," she said, half-choking.

That's when we met him.

The Marmoset Queen in the flesh.

He strutted through his animal-filled house with the air of a man who truly believed he was the ultimate authority on every living thing under his roof. The arrogance in his demeanor was palpable like we should have bowed before speaking.

"I've been doing this for years," he declared, puffing his chest out. "There's no one in the state who knows monkeys better than me."

We listened, nodding politely, as he rambled on and on. But when he turned away to grab something, my girlfriend and I locked eyes. Her look said everything: What the hell did we walk into? We didn't dare speak, but the unspoken conversation between our faces said it all.

This was the first time I realized something that would become painfully relevant as I continued in this business: what you see online is often a lie. This man had made himself look like a massive, respected breeder of monkeys. In truth? He had maybe eight or ten pairs of Marmosets. That was it.

I was still completely green, new to everything. I had no background in exotic animals, and no idea what to look for or what was normal. I was trusting.

Too trusting.

He suggested I buy baby marmosets from him and raise them into breeders. At the time, it sounded like a great way to get started. I had no clue that he was selling me two- or three-day-old babies.

Babies should be at least four to five weeks old before being separated from their mothers.

But I didn't know that yet.

What I did know was that we'd drive two hours home with the babies, and within a few days, some would start dying, two, sometimes three at a time. I didn't understand why. I was feeding them. Keeping them warm. Doing everything I thought was right.

When I called him about it, hoping for advice or support, he shrugged it off.

"That's your inexperience," he said, casually. "You're probably doing something wrong."

It didn't sit right with me.

Later, when I became more experienced, it all clicked. Those babies had no chance. They'd been taken from their mother far too early. He had used my ignorance for his financial gain. Nothing more.

But for the next three to four months, I kept going back. I'd pick up new babies, care for them until they were old enough, five or six weeks, and sell them. At least by then, I knew the right age to let them go.

One day, during a visit, he brought up something new.

"You ever think about getting a Capuchin?" he asked, casually sipping on some foul-smelling tea. "Got one just in. Real special. You'd love it."

I perked up. A Capuchin? I'd always wanted one. It was a high-priced primate, and I was thrilled at the idea of owning one personally.

"But don't you need some kind of license for that?" I asked, trying not to sound completely clueless.

"Oh sure," he replied, waving it off like it was a library card. "But don't worry, I've already prepared your hours."

"Hours?" I asked.

"Yeah, you need 1,000 hours of hands-on experience to qualify. I'll take care of it. Done this before."

That should've been a screaming red flag. But I was still new, still trusting. He made it sound perfectly normal. I thought he was doing me a favor.

What he was really doing was lining everything up for his payday. It wasn't about helping me. It was about making the sale.

On our way home, as usual, we talked about him. Sometimes we'd laugh at how absurd he was—the things he said, the way he acted like some animal messiah. Everything he taught me, diet, feeding, and care, was wrong. Absolutely wrong.

But I learned.

I may have started with zero experience, but one thing became crystal clear: I would never be anything like this man in my own business.

Eventually, I couldn't take it anymore. His arrogance. His lies. His manipulation. I had started meeting other people in the business, ethical people, and I began to see just how toxic his behavior truly was.

So I told him. Straight up. I told him what I thought of him.

It felt good.

I walked away from him and never looked back. Washed my hands clean of the Marmoset Queen. Good riddance.

I started working with better people and had better experiences. In just a few years, I was taking his customers. They left him willingly.

He didn't like that.

He got bitter. Petty. Started threatening people: "If you buy from him, I'll never sell to you again!"

The more I heard about his little tantrums, the more I laughed.

Meanwhile, my business was thriving. Growing. And I was doing it the right way.

To him, animals were just numbers. Commodities. Price tags.

But for me?

They weren't just animals. They were lives. And the one thing I promised myself from that point forward was that I would always lead with one thing, compassion, something the Marmoset Queen had none of.

Chapter 14
The Plunge, The Scar, The Surge

There are moments in life when the ground seems to crack open beneath your feet—when you're not sure if it's collapse or transformation. For me, that moment came in 2008, during a season that would change everything.

At the time, I was still buying breeder Marmoset monkeys, working my way deeper into the web of the exotic animal trade, meeting passionate breeders, collectors, and the occasional hustler. I called myself a "hobbyist breeder," not quite a business owner but definitely more than a casual enthusiast. I was dancing around commitment, flirting with the idea of turning passion into livelihood, but hadn't yet taken the plunge.

Meanwhile, I was still doing well in pest control sales. I was a proven closer, one of the best in my field. But the business model started to gnaw at me. Despite my strong sales, the company kept 75% of the earnings, and the more I succeeded, the more that split burned. I had the skill, the numbers, the demand, but not the control. And so, I made a decision that would split my life into before and after: I left pest control to enter the exotic animal business full-time.

It was a leap, and I knew there was no turning back. But failure? I didn't even entertain the thought.

I poured myself into expansion—building enclosures, refining my breeding practices, and setting up proper habitats. Everything I had learned from my time under the

"Marmoset Queen" came back into play. This time, though, I wasn't a student. I was the architect of my own future. I was confident. Focused. All-in.

Then life delivered a punch I never saw coming.

It started with a routine checkup at the Veterans Hospital. Just standard procedure. But when the chest X-ray came back, there was something off. Something suspicious. And from that moment, everything accelerated. It was like the world had pressed fast-forward.

Tests. Scopes. Appointments.

Diagnosis: lung cancer.

I heard those words with my mother sitting beside me. The pain in her eyes hurt more than the news itself. For two agonizing weeks, I lived under the weight of that word, cancer. I thought of the animals. The dream. The risk I had just taken. And the haunting possibility that I might not be around to see it through.

Three weeks after the X-ray, I was on the operating table. When I woke up, the surgeon approached and delivered a miracle: it wasn't cancer. A benign tumor was removed, along with half of my lung. But I would recover. I would live.

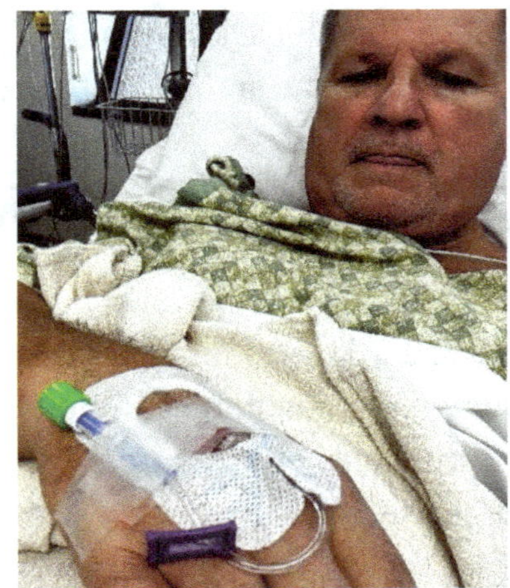

I felt like I had been born again. Grateful to God and thankful for another chance. A second wind, quite literally.

When I returned to my growing animal world, it was as if the near-death experience had ignited something even deeper. I wasn't just surviving, I was building something sacred.

Up until then, my only marketing had been a sign on my truck, one in my yard, and a modest Facebook presence. It was working, but barely.

Then one day, a potential customer stopped by. We got to talking—just a regular chat—but he said something that shifted my trajectory again:

"You should get a website."

He was a lawyer, and maybe that gave his suggestion a little more weight in my mind. I had thought about it before, but convinced myself it was too complicated, too technical. Still, I asked my girlfriend to help me figure it out.

And once again, everything changed overnight.

The website transformed me from a local, backyard monkey breeder into a nationwide presence. Calls started pouring in from every direction. Sure, many were time-wasters—dreamers, tire-kickers, people looking to "see a monkey" like it was a roadside attraction. But with every call, I was learning, Refining, and building a loyal customer base.

Even the nonsense calls had value, they kept me sharp and helped me understand what people wanted, what they were curious about, and what the market needed.

And while my name grew, so did my network. I was meeting new players in the industry, forming relationships, and making sure that every conversation, good or bad, moved the needle forward.

From a "hobbyist breeder" to entrepreneur, from a cancer scare to a second chance, from yard signs to national reach, this chapter of my life was a storm of decisions, disruptions, and divine direction.

But above all, it was the moment I stopped dancing around the edge and finally owned the fire inside me.

Chapters 15
Building the Dream, Facing the Cost

Things were going well for me in the exotic animal world. Every day brought a new lesson, a new challenge, a new reason to fall deeper in love with this wild, unpredictable life. I was constantly learning about species, care, habitats, and behaviors, and as I expanded my knowledge, I expanded my inventory. My collection of animals grew steadily, each addition carefully chosen and thoughtfully cared for.

As my experience grew, so did my network. I continued to establish connections with exotic animal keepers from coast to coast. These relationships weren't just casual exchanges; they became the backbone of my business and my support system. Through them, I gained insights, opportunities, and friendships that helped me shape a name for myself in a competitive world.

That name, my name, began to carry weight. I was doing consistent business with several animal people, and my reputation started to spread. I transitioned smoothly from being a recreational breeder to embracing the full-time role of a professional breeder. It was a significant shift, and one I felt proud of. I was finally comfortable in this new identity, rooted not just in passion but in purpose.

There's a moment when you realize you're becoming successful, and for me, that moment came the day someone stole my content and name online. It's funny, really. A twisted badge of honor. When scammers start using your photos and pretending to be you, you know you've officially arrived. It was frustrating, but also oddly validating. I laughed it off. Lol.

My yearly inspections were smooth—uneventful, really. I passed them easily. By that point, I had developed a routine. My animals were well-kept, their enclosures were clean, and my records were in order. There were no surprises, just confirmation that I was doing things right.

And I genuinely enjoyed having the animals. There was something deeply satisfying and endlessly fascinating about my interactions with them. The way they moved, the way they responded to me, the routines we developed — it never got old. Each animal had its own personality, and I valued them all.

Some of those animals were never going to make me money. They weren't profitable. They weren't flashy. But they were loved. I cared for them just like I did my top breeders. They had a home with me, and that was enough. Profit wasn't the only metric that mattered. Love and responsibility did, too.

By now, I was established. I had built something real, and people started noticing. I began to hear it more often: "You are living my dream life." It was flattering, but it also reminded me that people only saw the surface. They saw the animals, the success, the joy. But they didn't see the full picture.

Yes, this was my dream too, but it came with a cost.

One of the first signs of change came as animal rights groups like PETA started gaining more financial and political power. With that influence, they began pressuring regulatory agencies to take a tougher stance on exotic animal keepers. It was subtle at first — a tone shift, a harder look during inspections — but it was there. And it was growing. More on that later.

There were other downsides, too. As my collection of animals grew, so did the expenses. Feeding them wasn't cheap, and the larger the inventory, the heavier the burden. The workload increased. Every new mouth meant more time, more cleaning, more care. It was rewarding, but it was demanding.

And not all the challenges came from outside. Within the animal community itself, jealousy reared its head. Other keepers would talk behind my back, spreading rumors with no foundation. Lies. Pettiness. Envy masquerading as concern. It was disappointing, but not surprising.

Then there were the problem customers. You could give some people the moon, and they'd still complain about the stars. Some customers weren't just difficult — they were impossible. Even if I had given them the animal for free, they'd still find something to bicker about. They were unhappy long before they met me, I just became a new target for their dissatisfaction.

Through it all, I grew a thicker skin. That was necessary in this business. And early on, I made a decision I've never regretted: don't argue or debate with people on social media. It's not worth it. Nobody wins an argument on Facebook. It's just entertainment for people watching from the sidelines. I stayed out of the drama and stayed focused on my purpose.

It was around this time that an Egyptian friend introduced me to a Moroccan lady. That connection would come to mean more later. More on that soon.

Back home in Saint Petersburg, I was living on a corner lot, and I was out of space. Every square inch of my backyard was in use. Enclosures filled every corner. There was nowhere left to expand.

That's when I started thinking, maybe it's time for something bigger. A larger place. Somewhere in the country. Somewhere I could breathe. Somewhere, my animals could thrive.

Soon, I would find that place. A piece of paradise. A true sanctuary for me and for the animals I loved.

Chapter 16
From Oak Trees to Atlas Dreams

Life has a way of unfolding in the most unexpected places—and for me, it all began with ten acres of oak trees in a little town called Parrish. After years of operating as a small-scale breeder in my backyard, I reached a point where I knew it was time for a serious change. I wanted more for myself and more for the animals I loved and cared for. So, I hired a realtor and set my sights on properties in the next county.

That's when fate stepped in.

The realtor led me to a plot just outside Tampa, a quiet, almost forgotten town called Parrish. There, nestled among towering oak trees, sat a modest but charming three-bedroom house. The land sprawled across ten acres, a lush, green expanse that seemed to breathe with possibility. I wasn't alone on this trip. My cousin Chuck, a hardened Vietnam veteran with a good eye and grounded instincts, came along with me to scope it out. The moment we pulled up to the property, something shifted inside me. I fell in love with the trees, with the space, with the potential.

I pulled the trigger and bought it.

This move was more than just a real estate decision—it marked a turning point. I was no longer just a backyard breeder. Now, I had space, freedom, and opportunity. I rolled up my sleeves and got to work, immediately diving into the construction of proper enclosures and animal pens. There was a new energy coursing through me. Every nail I hammered, every fence I built, brought me closer to realizing the kind of life I'd dreamed of.

Before this, my collection was limited to small monkeys—creatures that required less space and simpler setups. But now, with ten open acres at my disposal, a whole new world was unlocked.

I began acquiring more exotic animals.

The first were kangaroos and wallabies, who quickly made themselves at home. They had room to run, play, and live freely in the open spaces. Then came a pair of sleek, slippery Asian otters—clever creatures with curious eyes and endless energy. My fascination with rare animals deepened, and I soon added various types of deer, including a tiny and elusive species from China called Muntjacs, the smallest deer in the world.

But I didn't stop there.

Next came antelopes: elegant Black Buck and, incredibly, the ultra-rare Bongo, a creature so majestic it seemed like it had stepped out of a dream. I also added lemurs to the mix—two different species, to be exact. The iconic Ring-tailed Lemurs with their raccoon-like tails and the colorful, vocal Ruffed Lemurs. These four—lemurs, deer, kangaroos, and otters—formed the core of my permanent breeding stock.

At any given time, the ranch buzzed with even more life—transient guests in the form of traded, bought, and sold animals. Anteaters ambled about with their long snouts; sloths hung lazily in their pens; African porcupines shuffled through their bedding. And then there was Humphrey, my personal camel and the uncontested mascot of the ranch.

Humphrey wasn't just any camel. He had a personality. He was affectionate, intelligent, and almost dog-like in his loyalty. To help him live up to his full potential, I called in my good friend Tim from Alabama, one of the most well-known camel trainers in the industry. Tim took Humphrey home for a time and worked with him closely, teaching him tricks and preparing him for rides. When Humphrey returned, he was a star—and he still is to this day. I love that animal-like family.

But the story of this chapter doesn't end on American soil.

Around the same time, through a group of Moroccan friends, I was introduced to a young woman named Hasnaa. She lived in Agadir, a city on the Atlantic coast of Morocco, and she was unlike anyone I'd ever met. Hasnaa was Muslim, a woman of discipline and grace. She had never smoked, never drank, and didn't even know what drugs were. She had jet-black hair, flawless olive skin, and a calming presence that drew me in immediately.

Something about her stirred my curiosity and my heart.

Though it was far outside my comfort zone, I booked a flight to Agadir. I'd never done something so impulsive in my life, but then again, I'd always had a thing for the exotic.

When I arrived, I learned that Hasnaa lived with her parents, a traditional arrangement in her culture. Meeting her family was nothing short of eye-opening. They were warm, respectful, and astonishingly kind. I had never been treated so well by people who were complete strangers. Their humility and graciousness made me feel like I belonged.

We spent days exploring Morocco together. We took a bus to Marrakesh, an ancient city that felt like a living tapestry of color, sound, and history. The bustling bazaar was surreal: cobras danced to flute music, monkeys sat beside their trainers, and spices wafted through the air. We rode camels through the Atlas Mountains, winding along rugged paths with panoramic views of the desert. We hiked to stone-carved cafes and dined under the stars.

That's where she truly captured my heart.

Eight months later, I returned to Morocco and married her.

Back at the ranch, while my heart adjusted to this newfound love, my reality was also shifting in a major way. Along with the joy of marriage and exotic animal companionship came an overwhelming workload. Ten acres of land sounds like paradise, and it is, but it's also relentless labor.

Between daily feedings, habitat maintenance, veterinary care, and planning for breeding and sales, I found myself in constant motion. I had always been a "ball of fire," full of energy and passion. But this was the greatest challenge I had faced yet. And somehow, I was ready for it.

I had love, land, a legacy, and a vision. And I wasn't slowing down.

Chapter 17
A Cast of Characters

When I look back now, I almost smile at how naïve I was in the beginning. Stepping into the world of exotic animals, I had stars in my eyes and the best of intentions. I believed everyone who shared this passion would be as honest and earnest as I was. But as the road unfolded, so did the masks—and the illusions I once held about people I admired began to dissolve.

At first, I was just another wide-eyed newcomer watching from the sidelines, admiring the "big names" in the exotic animal world, especially here in Florida. I watched them on social media, read their posts, followed their work, and imagined how amazing it would be to one day do business with them. But I'll say this much: be careful about meeting your idols. There is something incredibly disheartening about finding out the people you once held in such high regard are not who they appear to be.

Some of these so-called "big wheels" in Florida, whom I once respected deeply, ended up disappointing me the most. The deeper I got into business with them, the clearer it became—they were chasing paydays, not passion. I had people sell me sick animals, blatantly lie about an animal's age or health, and try to cut corners every chance they got. Their word meant nothing. Integrity was rare.

So, I learned, sometimes the hard way, who not to pick up the phone for. I earned a reputation as someone who did a lot of business, but I wasn't open to just anybody. I was selective, very selective. Over time, I formed an inner circle—people I could trust. And then there were the others: the ones on the outer edges, orbiting like satellites, always trying to slip into my world. Those were the people I had to watch like a hawk.

Yet, not everyone in this business was a disappointment. In fact, I met some of the most amazing people along the way. People who reminded me why I loved this life in the first place.

There was Kim, right here in my hometown of Saint Pete. Experienced, wise, and generous with her advice, Kim became a trusted friend. She helped me navigate many of the industry's tricky turns and never once led me astray.

Further north, in Tennessee, there were Jamie and Nancy Banes. They transported animals for me, but they did far more than just drive, they carried a deep and genuine love for animals in their hearts. We bonded over that love and became friends for life. To this day, I treasure our friendship.

In Georgia, Dwayne stood out as another gem. He had a world of knowledge and was always willing to share it. Whenever I had a question or needed a second opinion, Dwayne was just a call away, always honest, always wise.

Now, don't get me wrong, the exotic animal world, especially when it came to monkeys, was full of drama. You wouldn't believe the chaos. After my run-in with the infamous Marmoset Queen, though, I couldn't help but laugh at all the petty antics that came afterward. People formed little groups on Facebook, mostly just to gossip and badmouth one another. It was childish and toxic, and I wanted no part of it.

Amid all the business, lessons, and late-night drives, life kept happening. Beautiful things bloomed alongside the madness.

My son Dakoda and his wife brought two radiant new lights into my world: little Junebug and little Dakoda. My heart grew a whole new chamber for them.

My other son, Justin, and his wife gave me a darling granddaughter named Talia, a perfect little spark of joy.

And then, believe it or not, my granddaughter Liberty had a son of her own, making me a great-grandpa.

Can you believe that? A great grandpa! Life has a way of sneaking those surprises in when you least expect them.

So yes, this journey has been complicated. It's been full of lessons, betrayals, bonds, and blessings. But through it all, I've come to know who I am, who I trust, and what truly matters. And I wouldn't trade a single chapter.

Chapter 18
Sale Barn Shenanigans

Sale barns, better known to the average person as exotic animal auctions, are scattered all across the United States. These auctions are where breeders, collectors, and curious enthusiasts gather to buy and sell animals, often rare and sometimes bizarre. I've attended auctions in five different states, and though the locations may change, the format rarely does.

First off, let me say that I genuinely enjoy the auctions. There's an energy to them, a mix of commerce, chaos, and community. You feel it in the buzz of the crowd, the rapid-fire chant of the auctioneer, and the rustle of cages being wheeled in. It's a sensory overload, but an exciting one.

One of the best things about going to these auctions is the chance to reconnect with people I wouldn't otherwise see. We live in different states and lead different lives, but the sale barn is our meeting ground. Some of the animals I've bought there—mostly babies—have been among my favorites.

But with the good comes the bad. And at sale barns, there's plenty of both.

One of the most heartbreaking patterns I've seen involves baby animals, too young to be taken from their mothers, being sold off just to meet the auction schedule. Auctions often happen every two to three months, and some sellers fear they won't have another chance to offload their litters. So, they bring in underage babies, hoping someone will take them. It happens far more often than it should.

I've watched buyers—some experienced, some not take these animals home, unaware of just how fragile they are. Sometimes, the outcome isn't pretty. And sadly, by then, there's nothing anyone can do. The sale was final the moment the hammer dropped.

Then there's the deception. I've seen sellers bring in adult animals in one cage and, in another cage, place babies of the same species. The adult animals, usually a non-reproducing pair, are falsely advertised as "proven breeders," with the babies presented as their offspring.

The truth? Those babies often come from a completely different pair back at the facility.

"It's a proven pair!" the auctioneer will shout confidently. "Here are their babies to prove it!" The crowd stirs, bids fly, and someone walks away thinking they've scored a productive pair when really, they've been misled.

This tactic serves two purposes for the seller: they offload animals that don't reproduce, and they make more money in the process. The buyer, however, is cheated, plain and simple.

Is it the auctioneer's fault? Not really. He only repeats what the seller tells him. But let's not pretend the auctioneer is innocent either. Whether he's the barn owner or just a hired voice, his job is to drive excitement and maximize the money flowing through that ring.

As I like to say, an auctioneer is a salesman on steroids.

I'm not immune to the hype either. Once, I bought an American Buffalo.

Yes, a buffalo.

Did I need it? Absolutely not.

Did I get swept up in the adrenaline of the auction? Without a doubt.

There's a kind of spell that the auctions cast. You think you're bidding with your brain, but really, it's your ego, your excitement, your inner child that's calling the shots. And sometimes, that leads to regret, parked in your backyard chewing cud.

Another issue with these auctions is that they become dumping grounds for old or sick animals. Sellers lie about the animal's age to fetch a higher price. Some diseases don't show immediate symptoms, so buyers take home animals that seem fine, only to discover the truth days or weeks later.

Again, the buyer is left holding the bag. No returns. No refunds. Just lessons, often expensive ones.

Interestingly, the auction house doesn't always see every transaction. The real wheeling and dealing often happens outside, in the parking lot. Buyers and sellers meet there to avoid the barn's fees, making deals directly.

I'll admit it, I've done it myself. Everyone has. It's like a shadow market, running parallel to the official one. And while it cheats the sale barn out of their cut, it's often seen as just another part of the culture.

There's one story that still sticks with me, about a man whose name I won't mention. But those in the animal world will know who I'm talking about.

This guy would pick up imported animals from the Miami airport, often South American species not required to be quarantined. He'd get them a day or two before an auction, load them straight into his van, and head for the sale barn.

What's the problem, you ask?

The animals would be infested with parasites.

Within a week, many of them would die from the infections. But by then, the buyer's money was gone. The seller had already moved on, hidden behind the auction process. And because all sales were final, there was no way to get justice.

Despite all of this, I've met many decent, genuine people through the auction circuit. There's a certain camaraderie that exists among regulars. We exchange tips, swap stories, and sometimes even help each other avoid a bad buy.

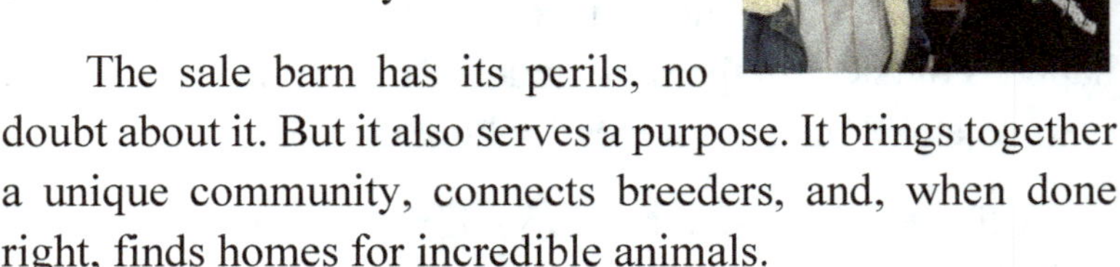

The sale barn has its perils, no doubt about it. But it also serves a purpose. It brings together a unique community, connects breeders, and, when done right, finds homes for incredible animals.

You just have to walk in with open eyes and a healthy dose of skepticism.

Because in a sale barn, everything has a price, even trust.

Chapter 19
The Chris Brown Incident

It was sometime in early 2021 when I sold a capuchin monkey to a woman from Virginia. She'd reached out after being referred by someone I'd worked with before. Her tone over the phone was pleasant but impersonal, the kind of transactional energy that wasn't uncommon in this line of work. Still, I made sure to vet her interests and intentions before proceeding. The monkey was healthy, well-socialized, and ready for rehoming under the proper conditions.

When we finalized the deal, I was told the handoff would take place in Las Vegas. I found that odd because she lived in Virginia, yet she didn't come to collect the monkey herself. Instead, she sent a team of transporters who carefully secured the monkey's carrier. I didn't think much about it again until a few days later when my phone buzzed with a headline that made my stomach drop.

"PETA Slams Chris Brown Over Illegal Monkey."

I blinked. Chris Brown? The Chris Brown? The article wasn't vague, it was a full-blown press release. Photos of the monkey, unmistakably the one I'd sold, sitting in the lap of Chris Brown's daughter. The pictures had gone viral after Brown posted over fifty shots to his Instagram, showing the little monkey clinging to toys, perched on his daughter's shoulder, curled up in her arms.

Almost immediately, California authorities descended upon Brown's home.

My heart pounded. "This can't be happening," I whispered, scrolling through the article as my phone trembled in my hand.

Within hours, the story was everywhere. TMZ, People, and even CNN ran it. PETA had seized the opportunity like a predator on wounded prey. They painted Chris Brown as reckless and unethical. But they didn't stop there, they aimed their sights squarely at the bigger picture: the private ownership of exotic animals in the U.S.

Chris Brown, whether knowingly or not, had become the latest pawn in their campaign. But I—I—was the one holding the bag.

The next week was a whirlwind.

Federal agents from the United States Fish and Wildlife Service contacted me. They came with questions—some friendly, some not. Then came the seizure. They wanted to see everything. Animal records, transport papers, correspondence. They walked out with boxes of files, and I watched the door close behind them, realizing just how serious things were about to become.

If this incident with the capuchin monkey had been the only issue, I would have stood my ground and fought it to the end. But during their review of my records, they discovered something else—three Cottontop Tamarins had been sold across state lines.

Apparently, that violated the Lacey Act.

Let me be clear: I had never heard of the Lacey Act. Not once. Not during my years in the animal trade. Not when I received my Federal USDA License. Not when I was handed their handbook, which everyone in the industry called the Bible.

That handbook never said a word—not one single word—about the Lacey Act. And yet, here I was, being told I had broken it.

I tried to explain that the buyers of the tamarins had assured me they were breeding. That, as far as I understood, put us in the clear. But bureaucracy doesn't care about nuance. They saw the transactions and the transport, and they slapped me with a federal charge.

It was crushing. I wasn't some backroom dealer. I had never ridden a sale, never ducked a regulation. I'd played by the rules—at least the ones I'd been given.

But now the rules were changing. Or worse, they were being weaponized—all because of the media buzz PETA stirred up using Chris Brown's fame.

"This is a paperwork violation," my attorney kept repeating. "It's not like you smuggled endangered species in suitcases."

But that didn't stop them from treating it like a federal crime spree.

I was fined $90,000. A staggering amount for what amounted to a regulatory oversight. They placed me under house arrest, slapped me on probation, and left a black mark on a record that had been clean for nearly three decades—save for a single DUI from 28 years prior. A DUI I took responsibility for and never repeated. I hadn't touched a drop of alcohol since.

I paid the fine. I complied with every order. And I kept possession of my animals.

Then came the next blow.

My USDA license was suspended for one year. They told me—promised me—that I could reapply when that year was up. So I waited. I followed every rule and every condition. I reapplied as instructed.

They denied me.

That was the moment the dam broke.

I hired an attorney to take action. "They lied," I told him. "They said I'd get it back. They told me this was temporary."

He nodded. "Then we're going to hold them accountable."

Meanwhile, Chris Brown wasn't taking it lightly either. He hired Mark Geragos, a high-profile attorney with a reputation for going head-to-head with the system. I didn't blame him. He was blindsided, too.

But here's the thing nobody talks about: how many others in the animal trade have done the same as me? Sold across state lines under good faith? Followed the handbook? Thought they were playing it safe.

None of them were prosecuted.

Just me.

That's when I realized this wasn't about justice. It was about making an example. About using someone—anyone—to drive home a political point. And in this case, it was me.

That capuchin monkey, that woman from Virginia, those Instagram photos—they'd set off a chain of events that would change the course of my professional life. But they didn't break me.

If anything, they taught me that in this business, you don't just deal with animals—you deal with agendas.

And sometimes, the most dangerous predator isn't the one with claws. It's the one holding a press release.

Chapter 20
PETA's Shadow Empire – The Battle for the Soul of Animal Ownership

I spent twenty years building my business in the animal industry. In the beginning, things were simple. I had one agency overseeing my operations and my inventory. They were respectful, helpful, and genuinely interested in the well-being of both the animals and the people who cared for them.

That first agency was the FWC, or Florida Fish and Wildlife Conservation Commission. Based right in Florida, they worked with us, not against us. They were tough when they had to be, but they understood our world. They treated us like professionals, and we treated them the same way. There was mutual respect.

But over time, things started to shift.

The next agency to enter the picture was the USDA, the United States Department of Agriculture. Their involvement added another layer of oversight, more paperwork, more inspections, and a very different tone. They weren't quite as approachable. There was a colder professionalism creeping in. Still, we complied because we had nothing to hide.

I had two federal and one state agency monitoring my every move, not three federal agencies. FWC is a state agency USDA in the United States Fish and Wildlife Service or federal agencies. They weren't communicating with each other. And most critically, they weren't friendly anymore.

Their tone had changed. They were suspicious, stern, and increasingly accusatory like I was a criminal instead of an animal caretaker. And this wasn't just happening to me. I wasn't alone. It was happening across the country, to countless others in the animal industry.

What once was a partnership between keepers and regulators was now an adversarial battlefield.

The animal industry, once filled with passionate, responsible caretakers, had quietly become one of the most regulated industries in the United States. The friction between animal professionals and the growing number of enforcers was intensifying.

And then the curtain got pulled back.

We began to realize something that, at the time, I never could have imagined. PETA, People for the Ethical Treatment of Animals, was pulling the strings from the shadows.

They weren't just lobbying from the sidelines. They were actively pressuring these agencies, sometimes publicly shaming them through media campaigns if they didn't come down aggressively on animal keepers. And it worked. Their tactics included negative press, strategic hit pieces, and coordinated media releases designed to embarrass agencies into action.

But here's what I want to make crystal clear.

In all my years of inspections, not one violation ever involved abuse or mistreatment of animals. My inspection reports speak for themselves.

There are no cheap exotic animals. This is a high-responsibility field. Most people in this business go out of their way, above and beyond the call, to ensure their animals are healthy, enriched, and thriving. We know the value of life in our care. Yes, like any industry, there are bad actors, and yes, some regulation is necessary.

But when regulation becomes weaponized, when it becomes a tool to shut down private ownership altogether, we're no longer dealing with regulation. We are dealing with ideology enforced by policy.

And this is PETA's goal.

They don't just oppose exotic animal ownership. They are against the private ownership of any animal, even dogs and cats. That's not a conspiracy. That's from their own literature. They oppose zoos. They oppose service animals that help the disabled. They see all forms of animal-human relationships as exploitation.

Their TV commercials, the ones that tug at your heartstrings with sad music and images of abused pets, are carefully curated propaganda. They're fundraising tools designed to make the public think they're something they're not.

To every animal lover out there, educate yourself on PETA's real agenda. Don't be manipulated by a sad song and a shaky camera shot.

PETA is not a grassroots volunteer organization. They are a well-funded political fringe group. They've infiltrated regulatory agencies, embedding their own people into positions of influence. That's why the agencies so often act as if they're answering to PETA and not to the American people.

Right now, they're pushing a bill in Congress called the Primate Safety Act. On the surface, it sounds noble. But in reality, it's designed to eliminate private primate ownership altogether.

The first time it was introduced, it failed. But like all ideologues, they don't stop. They'll keep pushing and pushing until they wear down the resistance and force it through.

If passed, this will be game-changing legislation, not just for primate owners but for every animal owner who values freedom, responsibility, and science-based care over ideological control.

And I want to say this clearly. I respect people's right to have opinions. I have strong ones of my own. But where I draw the line is when an organization like PETA uses the government to impose its beliefs on others. That is not democracy. That is coercion.

If people truly knew PETA's true intent, I believe their donations would dry up. Their influence would crumble. But until that happens, we animal owners need to stand up, speak up, and educate the public because we know more about animal care than any politically motivated organization ever will.

The real fight isn't just for ownership. It is for the right to care, to protect, and to preserve, without being treated like criminals for doing what we love.

Chapter 21
Neutralizing the Threat

There are moments in life when the wind shifts—when something deep in your soul tells you it's time to let go. April of 2025 was one of those moments for me.

My life had been nothing short of an exhilarating ride. Two decades in the exotic animal industry had taken me across wild landscapes, into the trust of remarkable creatures, and through some of the most incredible experiences I could have ever imagined. But the thrill that once lit my path had begun to dim—not because of the animals, but because of what the industry had become.

"I'm tired," I had said to Hasna one evening, staring out at the enclosure where our last several rested beneath the dappled sunlight. "Not of them. Never of them. Just of fighting people who've never set foot in my shoes."

She looked up from the sink, her hands pausing in the dishwasher. "You mean PETA again?"

I nodded slowly. "It's not just PETA. It's all of them. The regulators. The inspections. The constant fear that a knock on the door might mean another citation—or worse."

Hasna walked over, resting a hand gently on my shoulder. "We always said this life was about love. When it stops being that, maybe it's time to choose peace."

We didn't get into this business for conflict. We never wanted to be seen as criminals for caring. For me, raising and caring for exotic animals wasn't just a livelihood—it was a calling. But in recent years, it felt like the industry, especially in Florida, had become a battlefield.

They were coming for us, keepers, breeders, handlers. The laws kept tightening. The accusations kept flying. And behind every regulation was the unspoken threat: You're the villain now.

I remember sitting down and thinking, I do not want this for my son, Dakoda. He had been around these animals for a long time. Knew them by name. Helped feed, clean, and nurture. They were part of our extended family.

"I thought, I don't want this for you," I told him. "I don't want you spending the next ten years fighting battles I started." Dakoda had supported me during this war, and I appreciated that. He could see it was hurting me, and I was weary of spending all my time fighting with PETA and their minions at the FWC, USDA, and U.S. Fish & Wildlife over minor paperwork violations.

There was a moment of silence.

And so, I made the hardest decision of my life. In April 2025, I voluntarily rehomed my entire collection. Each animal, each heartbeat, found a new place to call home. And I knew I would miss them with everything in me.

I stood by the transport truck that final morning, watching the handlers load the last of our animals—our lemurs.

What followed was a strange calm. A stillness I hadn't known in years. No more compliance letters. No more unannounced inspections. No more being told how to care for the beings I had spent my life loving.

I had neutralized the threat.

It came at a huge financial and emotional loss. I simply could not tolerate another minute of their harassing tactics and threats. My son and I are converting our ranch into a wedding venue, something less stressful and more enjoyable. I'm going to take a few more vacations and have more family time. That is what's important in the end.

I want to say something, too, to the many loyal customers who stood by me through the years—to those who came back time and time again, who shared their stories and sent photos of animals they adopted from us, thriving and loved. I see you. I thank you. Your kindness didn't go unnoticed.

As this chapter ends in my life, I'm excited about the future, our new business, meeting new people, and having these agencies out of my life. They cannot say a word to me now.

This industry has always attracted passionate, devoted people. But people can only be pushed so far. The stress of constant legal threats, of being treated like a criminal for loving animals, wears on you. I've seen tempers flare. I've seen the pressure break people. I worry that a truly violent incident is around the corner.

And all of it, all of it, because agencies with unchecked power decided we don't deserve dignity.

Dispersing my animals wasn't just a choice. It was an act of self-preservation. My family and I had become targets in a war we never enlisted in. And without oversight, these agencies wield their power like a hammer, blind to who they're breaking.

Still, I look around now, and I see something else. I see peace. I see time—precious time—with my grandbabies, who are the light of my life. I see quiet dinners with Hasna. I see slow walks, Sunday drives, and laughter echoing through the house again.

I see freedom.

My mother, God bless her, always told me, "Don't let someone else's fear change your heart." She was the most important influence in my life, and her voice still echoes when I need it most.

So no, I won't let PETA or any other agency define who I am. I won't let their narrative be louder than my truth. My love for animals hasn't changed. But now, I love them from a distance. I'll remember the way they chirped and purred and sang, the way they trusted me, and how they made me a better man.

And I'll hold on to the one thing they never understood:

This was never just business.

It was always family.

www.ingramcontent.com/pod-product-compliance
Lightning Source LLC
Chambersburg PA
CBHW071202300726
48975CB00004B/1252